THIS WALKER BOOK BELONGS TO:

Anissa

Kisses and tickle from

your godfather Nicolas

Kiss also from little Nelle & Aude

For Naomi, Joe, Eddie,
Laura and Geraldine
M.R.

First published 1987 by
Walker Books Ltd
87 Vauxhall Walk
London SE11 5HJ

This edition published 2000

2 4 6 8 10 9 7 5 3 1

This book has been typeset in Trump Mediæval.

Printed in Hong Kong

British Library Cataloguing in Publication Data
A catalogue record for this book is
available from the British Library.

ISBN 0-7445-7765-9

MICHAEL ROSEN
ILLUSTRATED BY
QUENTIN BLAKE

Spollyolly-
diddlytiddlyitis
The Doctor Book

WALKER BOOKS
AND SUBSIDIARIES
LONDON • BOSTON • SYDNEY

Down at the Doctor's

Down at the doctor's
where everybody goes
there's a fat white cat
with a dribbly bibbly nose,
with a dribble dribble here
and a bibble bibble there,
that's the way
she dribbles her nose.

Down at the doctor's
where everybody goes
there's a fat black dog
with messy missy toes,
with a mess mess here
and a miss miss there,
that's the way
she messes her toes.

Down at the doctor's
where everybody goes
there's a fat red parrot
who everybody knows,
with a hi-de-hi here
and a how-de-how there,
that's the parrot
that everybody knows.

What If...

What if I went to the doctor's
and I was ill and I went into her little room
where she's got the toys in the corner
and she's lying on the bed
because she's ill
so she says,
"Hello, I'm really ill.
What's wrong with me?"

So I pick up the stethoscope
and the thermometer
and all the other things on her desk
and I'm supposed to know what to do with them...
and I do!

I do know,
I'm there with the stethoscope listening,
and I'm testing and feeling
        and I'm saying, "Well, Doctor,
        I'll tell you what's wrong with you.
        You've got spollyollydiddlytiddlyitis,"

and she says, "Have I?"
And I say, "What you need is
a bottle of Rottybottytex."

And she says, "Thanks, thanks a lot.
Look, I've got some other sick people here,"
and she opens up a cupboard
and hundreds of ill people
walk out of the cupboard

and I'm testing and measuring and listening
for hours and hours, and all the time
it was me who was ill.

Things We Say

Nat and Anna

Nat and Anna sat in the waiting room with Mum.

Anna said, "When I grow up I'm going to be a doctor."

Nat said, "When I grow up I'm going to be a doctor."

Anna said, "I don't want you to be a doctor."

Nat said, "You can't stop me. Look, I'm a doctor."

Anna said, "No, you're not. You're Nat."

Nat said, "I'm Doctor Nat, the doctor."

Anna said, "So? I'm Doctor Anna."

Nat said, "I'm the doctor round here. You can be a lorry driver."

Anna said, "I don't want to be a lorry driver."

Nat said, "You can be ill. You've got a headache."

Anna said, "I'm not playing this anymore, Nat."

Nat said, "I am. I'm Doctor Nat. I'm Doctor Nat."
Anna said, "You're not. You're Doctor Sick
because you're sick all the time."
Nat said, "I'm not sick all the time."
Anna said, "Doctor Sick Sick Sick."
Nat said, "You're getting really ill, Anna, and
I'm going to make you better."

Nat sat on Anna.

Anna said, "I'm not ill, I'm not ill, I'm not ill."
Mum looked up.
Mum said, "You are ill, Anna. That's why we've
come to see the doctor, okay?"

Nat said, "Anna is Doctor Sick."
Anna said, "Next time you're ill, Nat,
I'm going to be Doctor Jump and I'm
coming to jump on you."
Nat said, "Oh don't, Anna."
Anna said, "Yes, I will. Jump jump jump all over you."
Nat sat and thought about Anna jumping on him.
Nat said, "Hey, Anna. Look, let's both be ill, eh?"
Anna said, "No, let's both be Doctor Jump."

Feeling ill

Lying in the middle of the bed
waiting for the clock to change
flicking my toes on the sheets
watching a plane cross the window
staring at the glare of the light
smelling the orange on the table
counting the flowers on the curtain
holding my head with my hand
hearing the steps on the stairs
lying in the middle of the bed
waiting for the clock to change.

This Woman Went to the Doctor's

This woman went to the doctor's and she said,
"Doctor, my family, we keep thinking we're all
  sorts of different things."
"Like what?" said the doctor.
"Sometimes I feel like a cat."
"When did you start feeling like this?" said the
  doctor.
"When I was a kitten," she said.

"Oh, yes," said the doctor. "Anything else?"

"Well, my husband," she said, "he thinks he's
  a bell."

"Ah," said the doctor, "tell him to give me a ring.
  Anyone else?"

"Yes," said the woman, "my little boy. He thinks
  he's a chicken."

"Why didn't you tell me this before?" said the
  doctor.

"We needed the eggs," said the woman.

"Any other problems?" said the doctor.

"Yes, I keep forgetting things."

"What did you say?" said the doctor.

"I don't know," said the woman. "I've forgotten."

Spollyollydiddlytiddlyitis

MICHAEL ROSEN says, "What a clever fellow Quentin Blake is! I came to Walker Books one day and Quentin was sitting there with a scrappy piece of paper. On it was written a list of ideas: jokes, riddles, conversations, poems, things to do, cartoons … and that's how these books (pictured below) came about. When I was a kid one of my favourite books was *The News Chronicle I-Spy Annual*. It would last me the whole year. I hope my series does the same for kids today."

Michael Rosen is one of the most popular contemporary poets and authors of books for children. His titles include *We're Going on a Bear Hunt* (Winner of the Smarties Book Prize), *This Is Our House* and *Little Rabbit Foo Foo*. He also compiled *Classic Poetry: An Illustrated Collection*. He's a regular broadcaster on BBC Radio and in 1997 received the Eleanor Farjeon Award for services to children's literature. Michael Rosen lives with his family in London.

QUENTIN BLAKE says, "I have always liked Michael Rosen's poems; and what I particularly enjoy when I am illustrating them is that he seems to know everything about everyday life, but at the same time there is some fantasy that gets in as well."

Quentin Blake consistently tops all polls as the most popular children's book artist. The illustrator of numerous Roald Dahl titles and several Michael Rosen poetry collections, he has also created many acclaimed picture books of his own, including *Mr Magnolia* (Winner of the Kate Greenaway Medal), *The Green Ship* and *Zagazoo*. In 1999 he was appointed the first Children's Laureate. He lives in London.

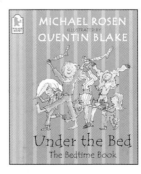

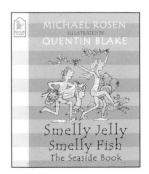

ISBN 0-7445-7764-0 (pb)   ISBN 0-7445-7765-9 (pb)   ISBN 0-7445-7763-2 (pb)   ISBN 0-7445-7766-7 (pb)